DOUBLE TAKE

Adapted by Marianne Schaberg

Based on the series created by Michael Curtis & Roger S. H. Schulman

Part One is based on the episode, "That Ding You Do!" Written by Heather MacGillvray & Linda Mathious

Part Two is based on the episode, "Beauty and the Beat," Written by Kevin Kopelow & Heath Seifert

DISNEP PRESS

New York

Printed in the United States of America

First Edition
1 3 5 7 9 10 8 6 4 2
J689-1817-1-09288

Library of Congress Catalog Card Number: 2009920717
ISBN 978-1-4231-1621-9

For more Disney Press fun, visit www.disneybooks.com
Visit DisneyChannel.com

PART
ONE

CHAPTER ONE

It was just a typical afternoon in the Lucas household. Kevin, Nick, and Joe were lounging in their living room together. Their living room, however, *wasn't* so typical.

The boys lived in a converted firehouse with their parents and younger brother, Frankie. Having to slide down a pole to reach the breakfast table wasn't the only thing that set the three Lucas brothers apart from other teenagers—they also happened to be mega rock stars. They were so famous that their pictures were plastered on the walls of rooms everywhere. Together, the three brothers made up the hottest rock band on the planet, JONAS.

That afternoon, Kevin, the oldest member of JONAS, was working on his pecs, lifting twenty-pound weights in the corner. He needed to stay fit if he was going to jam out practically every night onstage. Nick sat on a stool strumming his guitar, practicing a new song for the band. Sprawled out on the couch, Joe wasn't working quite so hard; he was reading a magazine.

"Hey, guys, check it out. There's a 'How Well Do You Know JONAS?' quiz in the new *Teenster* magazine!" Joe called out, flipping to a page in the magazine. He always got a kick out of the questions—and answers. "Let's see how well I know . . . Joe!"

Joe went through each question aloud: "Yes . . . No . . . Yes . . . No . . . Armadillo."

Clutching the magazine, Joe jumped up

on the couch. "Five out of five! I'm a . . ." He searched for his score. "'Real Joe Nut,'" he read.

Curious, Kevin and Nick walked over to check out the quiz. Reading over Joe's shoulder, Nick raised an eyebrow. "Hey, your favorite snack isn't cherry pudding," he said to Kevin.

Kevin shook his head. "It's chocolate tacos. And your favorite color isn't medium spring green," he told Nick as he flopped down on the couch, dejected.

"It's electric indigo," Nick said, frowning.

Pulling the magazine away from Joe, Kevin read his profile. Everything was wrong! This meant war! "We need to straighten out *Teenster* magazine!" he cried.

Excited by the prospect of putting the magazine in its place, Kevin turned toward his brothers and went on. "You know what? We need to write them a letter," he said and searched for the editor's name in the magazine. "Anybody got a pen?" he asked his brothers.

Fumbling through his pockets, Nick shook his head. No luck.

Within seconds, Joe had a solution. "Hold on," he said. He jumped up and ran over to one of the windows in the living room.

As soon as he opened the window, the sound of hundreds of screaming fans poured into the firehouse. On a daily basis, fans surrounded the Lucas home, patiently waiting for just one peek at the band. This caused serious problems for the boys and their family. They couldn't even buy groceries without getting swarmed.

Bracing himself, Joe peeked his head out the window. The sound rose to a deafening roar. Putting his hands up to his mouth, Joe shouted, "Excuse me, girls! Does anybody have a pen?"

As soon as the words left his mouth, a blizzard of pens came flying through the window. "Incoming!" Joe called as he ducked. Turning around, he saw the pens sticking out of the wall in a perfect heart-shaped pattern. Those fans had pretty good aim. Joe stood up. "Our fans are the best," he said to his brothers.

"And freakishly accurate," Nick pointed out, eyeing the heart made of pens.

Shutting the window, Joe walked over to the pens, pulled one out of the wall and sat down with his brothers to write a strongly worded letter to the editor.

CHAPTER TWO

At school the next day, Stella Malone and her friend, Macy Misa, were walking to class together. Stella was not only the best friend of the JONAS boys, she was also their stylist. It was a job any girl would want, but it kept her pretty busy— not that she complained . . . usually. It just meant she had to use her spare time wisely. Right now she was catching up on her backlog of text messages. She was in her own little world, her blond head bent over her phone.

Macy was in her own world, too: the world of JONAS. She lived and breathed JONAS. Despite having gone to school with the Lucas brothers for years, she still had a tendency to melt into a pile of mush whenever she saw, heard, or even smelled them.

"As president of the JONAS fan club, I'm trying to decide which new JONAS picture to post on the JONAS fan club Web site." Macy paused to take a much needed breath. "Help me pick?" she asked Stella.

Reading one of her texts, and completely ignoring Macy's JONAS report, Stella exclaimed, "Yes!"

Oblivious to Stella's distraction and happy for the help, Macy broke out a set of brand-new JONAS photos. "Pouty and intense JONAS?" Macy asked, flipping through the pictures of all the guys looking seriously handsome. Whipping out more photos, she gushed, "Or goofy and adorable JONAS?"

Stella still hadn't heard a single thing. Typing furiously into her phone, she didn't even look up.

Macy looked over at her friend for an answer.

Still reading her texts, Stella smiled. "Ms. Sherman just barfed all over the desk and went home sick—no algebra test today!" she said, delighted.

Macy's eyes grew wide. Wait a minute! Stella hadn't been paying attention to a word she said! Macy couldn't believe it. "You weren't even listening to me!" she cried.

Stella shrugged. "I don't have to listen to you," she pointed out. "You say the same thing every day. 'JONAS, JONAS, JONAS.'" Her fingers continued to rapidly press keys as she spoke. Being a stylist, a student, *and* a best friend to rock stars had made her pretty good at multitasking. "You can't go two seconds without talking about them," she said.

Macy sighed. She couldn't very well argue the fact. "Well, we all have our obsessions," she said.

"Except JONAS. They are *so* mentally fit," she added, a dreamy look in her eyes.

"*I* don't have any obsessions," Stella said matter-of-factly, pressing SEND.

"What are you talking about?!" Macy asked in disbelief. Was Stella joking? She'd been obsessing over her phone for the last ten minutes! "Look at you. You're addicted to texting. Your thumbs are turning into tiny sumo wrestlers."

Stella wasn't buying it. "I am *not* addicted to texting. I can give it up anytime. In fact, I bet I could go longer without texting than you could go without mentioning JONAS."

Always up for a challenge, Macy smiled. "Bet," she said, nodding her head.

Half thinking that Macy was kidding, Stella asked, "And the winner . . . ?"

Macy looked at Stella, her expression dead serious. "Wins." This was no joking matter; Macy was ready to show her best friend what she was capable of.

Sensing that her friend meant business, Stella

put on her game face. "You're on. Starting in . . . five seconds," she said, texting frantically.

"JONAS, JONAS, JONAS, JONAS," Macy chanted as the seconds ticked by.

With a tap of the SEND button, Stella took a deep breath. It was showtime. "GO!" she cried.

Setting their jaws determinedly, the girls continued walking to class. But things were not right. Stella didn't know what to do with her thumbs and shoved her hands into her pockets; Macy was suddenly stumped for a conversation topic. They both already missed their obsessions dearly. This was going to be a lot harder than they had thought.

CHAPTER THREE

Walking down the stairs of the Horace Mantis foyer, unaware of any challenges or bets that involved the name of his band, Joe came to a sudden stop. Kevin and Nick, who were behind him, slammed directly into his back and promptly fell down. Ouch.

Nick groaned. What had made Joe stop short on the busy stairwell? Maybe he was thinking of a new song lyric, or about what to have for lunch, or maybe he had just remembered that he'd forgotten a history assignment. Following Joe's gaze through the atrium window, Nick got his answer. There was no new lyric or misplaced homework assignment. There was a very beautiful girl standing in the atrium. *She* was what had stopped Joe in his tracks. Beside him, Nick saw Kevin make the connection, too. They should have known.

By this time, Joe was pressed up against the glass, peering into the atrium. The girl was passionately playing a cello. Nick and Kevin picked themselves up, collected their books, and walked over to join Joe.

The middle Lucas brother was one hundred percent smitten. "Look at her," Joe said, sighing. "Have you ever seen anyone *so* beautiful? Look at how she plays. Such passion. Punch me in the arm so I know I'm not dreaming!"

Typical Joe, Nick thought. He had seen this once, twice . . . no, make that close to at least fifty times before. He gladly socked Joe in the shoulder as hard as he could.

His gaze still fixed on the girl, Joe rubbed his shoulder. "Not dreaming, because that really hurt."

"Unless," Kevin said, "you're *dreaming* that it hurt, so that was a dream-hurt."

Joe wasn't even paying attention. He watched as the girl finished playing and started packing up her cello. Quickly, he checked his reflection in the glass. Hair? Perfect. Teeth? Sparkling. Shirt? Rockin'. Joe gave himself a quick thumbs-up. He looked good.

Kevin rolled his eyes. Here we go again, he thought. Zero to totally crushing in point five seconds.

Amused, Nick and Kevin watched as Joe fixed his trademark ascot and approached the cellist as she walked out of the atrium. Depending on his dashing good looks and kickin' style, he decided to go for a simple approach. "Hi," he said.

"Hi," the girl replied, her voice emotionless.

Not the reaction Joe had been hoping for,

but he wouldn't give up. "Can I carry that for you?" he asked.

"Sure," the girl replied.

Joe picked up the cello case. It felt as if he'd just lifted an SUV. "Have you considered wheels?" he asked, trying not to let the cello crush him.

The girl was used to lugging around her beloved cello and just laughed in response.

Shifting the case around to his back, Joe tried again. "So, what's your name?" he asked.

"Angelina."

Joe twisted his body once more, readjusting the massive instrument. "Angelina. Like *angel* with an *ina* on the end," he said, giving her his most charming smile.

Angelina was impressed—a little bit. She had never heard that one before.

"Yeah, my mom calls me Annie-Bug. My little sister calls me Annie-Bo-Banny. But most people call me Angie." Apparently, she was over the monosyllabic answers. Pausing, she asked, "What's your name?"

Joe practically dropped the cello. Had he heard right? How could *she* not know who *he* was? "Really?" he asked, utterly flabbergasted.

Angelina shrugged. "Well, you know mine." Who did this guy think he was? she wondered. Captain of the lacrosse team? Student body president? It was just a simple question.

"Joseph," Joe said, trying his best to sound smooth. "Joe for short. My brothers call me Danger. My mom, she calls me Joe-Bear." Then, leaning in, he added, "But that's just between us. I don't want that leaking to the media."

"The media?" Angelina was puzzled. What high-school student had to worry about that? Wait a second. . . . Of course! It all made sense now. Angelina knew Joe looked familiar—and not just from around the halls at school. She'd seen him on the cover of *Teenster* magazine; her little sister had a subscription.

"Oh, I know who you are! You're one of those brothers in that band that goes here," she said, not sounding all that impressed. Angelina knew the Lucas brothers were in a band and that almost all the girls in school were crazy about them. But she seldom gave them a second thought.

Joe put down the cello case. "Yup, JONAS," he said, leaning heavily against the case. "Me, Kevin, and Nick—the guys staring right at us." He pointed over at his brothers.

Noticing that the attention was suddenly on them, Nick and Kevin tried to act casual. Kevin quickly leaned against a locker, averting his eyes and whistling. Nick picked up a book and started to read it. It would have looked perfectly natural, only the book was upside down.

Still playing it cool, Joe asked, "So, do you want to grab something to eat sometime?"

"No thanks," Angelina said simply.

There had to be some mistake—girls didn't turn down Joe Lucas. "Why . . . don't you eat?" he asked, confused.

Angelina tried to break it to him gently. "Look, you're famous. You have a posse," she said, pointing at Nick and Kevin, who once again tried to look normal. "You probably play to thousands of screaming fans."

"Tens of thousands," Joe said proudly. "Isn't that cool?"

Angelina frowned. "Not really . . . I just don't go out with rock-star types." She shrugged apologetically.

She had to be kidding. Joe was totally down-to-earth. Sure, he and his brothers were on magazine covers, but they still had to do chores at home! Their mom actually insisted they be like other teenagers. "But I'm a *nice* rock-star type," Joe said, pleading.

It was too late. The bell rang, and Angelina was in motion.

"I have orchestra," Angelina said, picking up the cello case as if it were as light as a feather. Then without another word, she walked away.

When the coast was clear, Nick and Kevin quickly joined their brother.

"*Sooo*, are you going out with cello girl?" Kevin inquired.

Joe looked up at his brothers sadly. "No," he said. "She says because I'm a rock star, I must be some kind of jerk." His ego was thoroughly deflated.

"What?" Nick asked, completely confused. "In my experience, girls like guys *because* they're rock stars," he pointed out.

Kevin chimed in, "Sometimes I think that's the *only* reason girls like me. Well, that and my boyish charm," he added, winking at Joe.

Joe sighed. He knew his brothers were trying to help, but they just weren't getting it.

"Guys, this is serious. I think I like her. Like, *like* her like her," Joe told them.

"Really?" Kevin asked.

"Like, yeah," Joe replied sadly.

Understanding the gravity of the situation, Kevin asked, "Like, really *like* her like her?"

"Like, *really* like her like her," Joe answered gravely.

His brothers' eyes grew wide. It wasn't every day that Joe Lucas *like*-liked a girl. And *really* like-liking a girl who didn't *like*-like you back was a problem.

There was no time to lose. Nick knew that his brother was hurting. He wrapped an arm around Joe's shoulders. "All right. Then we'll help you show her the sweet, down-to-earth, panda-loving guy you really are," Nick said comfortingly.

"I do love pandas," Joe said.

"I love koalas," Kevin chimed in. "They're so emo. They eat all that eucalyptus, so their breath is minty-fresh."

"Unlike yours," Nick said.

"What?" Kevin asked, confused.

"Trust me," Nick told him as Joe passed Kevin a mint. The bell rang again. As they headed to class, Nick was already plotting how to turn things around for Joe and Angelina.

CHAPTER FOUR

Unaware of the latest Lucas brothers' drama, Stella and Macy were dealing with their own drama. As she waited for the elevator, Stella's thumbs fidgeted in her belt loops. What was the point of having thumbs if you couldn't text with them? she thought, fuming. Macy stood next to her, racking her brain for something to say that didn't include the letters *J, O, N, A,* or *S.*

It was hard. "I saw this excellent new JO—" Macy began.

"I'm sorry, JONAS what?" Stella asked, seizing the opportunity to bust her friend.

Ack! She had almost blown it! Quick on her feet, Macy caught herself. "JO-gging suit. You know, for when I go JO-gging."

Ding. The elevator door opened. Phew. Content with her cover-up, Macy walked into the elevator. Stella followed, disappointed that she hadn't gotten her friend to crack. She was beginning to wonder how much longer she could go without texting!

The girls stood silently in the elevator, lost in their own thoughts. Macy's mind, of course, began to wander to JONAS. Joe, Nick, and Kevin. Nick, Kevin, and Joe. Kevin, Joe, and Nick. Seriously, what else was a girl supposed to think about?

"I love those T-shirts I saw Ni—" Macy caught herself again and quickly shut her mouth.

Stella grinned. It hadn't even been a minute,

and already she had another chance to catch Macy in a JONAS trap. "*Ni*-who?" she teased.

"Oh, *Ni-ooo*body," Macy said. That was a close one!

Stella was on the verge of winning, she just knew it. She could almost feel her cell phone in her hand again! But she couldn't leave it to chance. She had to take the offensive. She had to force Macy to fold.

"It's just a matter of time before you say something about JO-*NAYS*," Stella said, hoping that Macy would take the bait.

Macy looked at Stella, her mouth open. How could her friend mispronounce the name of the greatest band in the history of the world?! This was ridiculous. Ludicrous. "It's pronounced JO—" Macy began. Wait a minute . . . She saw what Stella was up to. "Nice try," she said and smiled, proud of her catch. But then she sighed. She had come dangerously close to being tricked . . . again! "How is this so easy for you? I'll bet you're closet texting!" Macy complained.

"No," Stella replied matter-of-factly. "I just happen to have willpower. And just to ease your suspicious mind, why don't you hold on to this." She pulled out her phone and handed it to Macy.

Macy quickly snatched it out of Stella's hands and put it in her own purse. "You're going to break," she said, feeling more certain now that she had taken Stella's phone captive.

"*Nuh*-uh. Without my little phone screen to stare at, I'm seeing so much more of the world, and it's . . . beautiful. . . ." Stella trailed off and then looked at Macy as if she were seeing her for the first time.

"Macy, you have brown eyes! *And* a little something in your teeth," Stella pointed out as the elevators doors opened. Waiting to enter was a member of the basketball team. A very cute member. Mortified, Macy quickly covered her mouth with her hand. This day was getting worse by the minute!

CHAPTER FIVE

The plan to capture Angelina's heart was about to be set in motion. Kevin and Nick were on the lookout while Joe stood by his locker, trying different poses. Should he lean against the locker? Cross his arms? Put one hand in his pocket? Both hands? While Joe's brain raced, he kept one eye on his brothers, awaiting their signal.

Meanwhile, Nick and Kevin huddled together, going over their plan one more time. "Okay,"

Nick said, "when we see Angelina, we give Joe the signal."

Demonstrating, Nick performed an elaborate hand gesture that looked like something a baseball catcher would do.

Kevin felt as if his head were spinning. Didn't Nick know that a signal should be simple?

"What if the signal is that we stand completely still?" Kevin suggested. He demonstrated, standing as still as a mannequin, complete with a vacant look in his eyes.

Nick scoffed. "What kind of a signal is that?" he demanded.

"The best kind," Kevin responded, "because it's so subtle, no one will even know that it's happening." Again, Kevin struck a lifeless pose, staring off into space.

Nick immediately looked around for Angelina, thinking Kevin was doing the signal for real this time. "Is that the signal? Is she coming?" he asked frantically.

Kevin came back to life and smiled proudly.

"No, I'm just demonstrating."

Nick relaxed. "How am I supposed to know the difference between the signal and when you're just standing still?" he asked his brother.

"True," Kevin said. "Okay, when I do this"—he began to wave his arms around like a crazed fan at a baseball game—"is when I'll give the signal, which is this. . . ." He froze again in midwave.

Kevin's complicated signal was beginning to look like an air-traffic-control robot dance. As he performed the routine, Angelina walked by Nick and Kevin—without them even noticing.

Angelina opened her locker, then paused. Something struck her as out of place. Her schedule of orchestra practices, usually stuck to the locker door with an "I ♥ MOZART" magnet, fell out when she opened the door. Something was definitely not right.

Taking a closer look at her locker, she saw a magazine stuck in the vents. It was clearly not hers—it was a copy of *Teenster* magazine. And JONAS was staring her right in the face.

She held the magazine in her hand and closed the locker door . . . only to find a member of the band right in front of her.

"How did this magazine get in my locker?" Angelina asked Joe, her eyes narrowing suspiciously.

How had it gotten in there? Simple. About fifteen minutes earlier, Joe had shoved, stuffed, pushed, prodded, and poked that magazine through the vent. It had been no easy task. He had worked up quite a sweat and ruined a perfectly good fork.

"I have no idea," Joe said, trying to sound innocent. Angelina's eyes narrowed even further.

Ignoring her gaze, Joe took the somewhat tattered magazine. "But take a look!" he said as if surprised. "On the cover it says, 'Joe of JONAS, a Regular Guy.' And there's a picture of me bowling in rental shoes. Size nine, *regular*."

Angelina wasn't fooled. Nor was she even impressed. "*Regular* people don't have their faces on the cover of magazines," she pointed out.

This was not how things were supposed to go. Just as Joe was beginning to panic, Stella and Macy came into view. If there was anyone who knew what a "regular Joe" Joe was, it was Stella. Maybe she could help him!

Like a drowning man grabbing a life vest, Joe quickly grabbed Stella before she could pass. "Stella!" he said. Then he turned to Angelina. "This is my friend Stella. We've been best friends since I was three." He turned back to Stella. "Stella, can you please tell her what a regular guy I am?"

Unfortunately for Joe, he was about to get caught in the middle of Stella and Macy's battle. In fact, Stella barely registered his question. Instead, she saw a perfect opportunity to push Macy over the edge. Macy already looked wobbly just from being so close to Joe Lucas. With the right move, Stella would win and be back to texting in no time.

Smiling sweetly, Stella turned to Macy and pushed her closer to Joe and Angelina. "Macy, why don't *you* tell her?" she suggested to her friend.

Wobbly knees were only the beginning. Macy's eyes were as wide as a deer's in headlights, and she was pretty sure air was no longer reaching her lungs. Joe Lucas was right in front of her!

Mustering all the strength she could, Macy collected herself. "I—I don't know who you are, mister!" she stammered.

Unfortunately, she wasn't *completely* collected. She almost choked and swallowed her gum. Macy knew she was losing this battle—she couldn't help it. Every fact about Joe Lucas started to flood her mind—his favorite movie, what condiments he liked on his hamburger, which shoe he put on first in the morning. They were bubbling up in Macy's throat. She was like a volcano ready to explode. . . .

"I don't know that you're a giant rock star," she went on. "And that you wear size nine regular bowling shoes. Leave me alone!" she cried, before turning bright red and running away.

Stella couldn't contain her excitement. She began jumping up and down. She was a breath away from winning. Macy would say JONAS soon, she just knew it. "Classic Macy," she said as she started to rummage through her purse, itching to text the news to just about everyone on her contact list.

"I can't wait to tell—" she began, but then she remembered: Macy had her cell phone! Stella felt like she'd been socked in the stomach. She trudged off, mumbling under her breath, "No phone. No life . . ."

Angelina could hardly believe what she'd just witnessed. Not only was Joe Lucas a rock star, but his friends also seemed to be . . . well . . . rather unstable. She shook her head.

"This isn't going well for me, is it?" Joe asked, smiling meekly.

"Look, Joe," Angelina said. "Last year I went out with a guy who was also a star. He was a champion mathlete. All I would do was replace the batteries in his calculator and sharpen his pencils. I don't want to go there again." She stopped talking and looked at him expectantly.

"I would never be like that!" Joe argued. "I hate calculators, and I don't even have a pencil."

Suddenly pencils started flying out of nowhere. When the barrage stopped, there was a heart in the wall made of pencils. Joe gulped. His fans were *not* helping the situation.

"I just think it wouldn't work out between us," Angelina said, shaking her head. Then she turned and walked away.

Joe was crushed. He'd tried everything he could think of, and Angelina just would not budge.

"But . . . I *like*-like you," Joe whispered as he watched Angelina continue down the hall, turn the corner, and possibly walk out of his life forever.

CHAPTER SIX

Nick and Kevin returned to their bedroom after school to relax before starting their homework. Their room, like the rest of the converted firehouse where the Lucases lived, was awesome. It even had bunk beds designed to look like the ones on the JONAS tour bus. As the boys dropped their backpacks, they heard a low groan from one of the beds: Joe's.

Curious, Nick walked over. Joe was curled

up in his pajamas with hundreds of letters from fans. Whenever Joe was feeling particularly down, he found solace in fan mail. Seeing the amount of letters, Nick groaned. This was not good.

Joe propped himself up. "Look," he said. "Amy from Boise writes: 'Joe, even though we've never met, I know you're a very kind and generous person.'" He looked over at his brothers. "And she'd know, because look how she signed it: 'X-O-X-O'"—Joe had to flip the letter over to continue—"'X-O, heart, heart, smiley face!'" Joe proudly showed his brothers the signature.

Joe needed to get a grip. "I know you like Angelina," Nick said gently. "But she's just one girl." Taking a moment to think about it, he added, "Unless she has an identical twin, in which case, I am mistaken and I apologize."

Kevin was a little more blunt. "Dude, it's time to move on," he said.

Joe put his hands over his face. He was in

agony without Angelina. How could anyone suggest that he "move on"?!

"I don't want to move on. I've never met a girl like her. She's passionate and talented *and* beautiful!"

As Joe declared his devotion to Angelina, the boys' father, Tom Lucas, walked into the room.

"Who's 'passionate, talented, and beautiful'? Besides your *mother* . . ." Mr. Lucas said the last word quite loudly as he shot a quick look toward the fire poles, which led downstairs. "She can hear everything through those holes," he whispered to his sons.

Joe sat up. "This girl at school," he told his father. "She thinks because I'm a rock star, I must be some kind of jerk."

Mr. Lucas frowned. "Your mom and I have worked pretty hard to make sure you *didn't* turn into some kind of 'rock-star jerk,'" he told Joe. "And if I do say so myself, I think we've done pretty well with all you boys."

Joe knew his dad was trying to help but he

was still frustrated. "It's just that she won't even come within a mile of me."

Mustering up all the fatherly advice he could, Mr. Lucas went on. "No, she won't come within a mile of the person she *thinks* you are, but you're really not who she thinks you are. Just be yourself, and she'll realize she's wrong."

Joe nodded. His dad was right. He wasn't going to make any progress until he could really show Angelina how down-to-earth he was. It was time to take serious action.

Mr. Lucas gave his son a quick pat on the back. "Even if you do just the littlest thing, a woman will appreciate it," he advised. Looking toward the fire poles again, he raised his voice. "Because women are *perceptive, sensitive, and intelligent!*"

On the other side of the bed Nick rolled his eyes, knowing exactly what his father was doing. "Dad, Mom is at the park with Frankie."

CHAPTER SEVEN

The Horace Mantis orchestra room was full of students warming up their instruments. Mr. Phelps, the orchestra leader, was cautiously watching over everyone, giving pointers when needed. They had a performance coming up, and he wanted everything to go perfectly.

Angelina was busy playing a melody on her cello, when Joe Lucas walked in and waved at her. What was *he* doing here? Rock stars didn't play in the orchestra! Angelina ignored his presence and kept playing.

Joe might not have had an effect on Angelina, but he had an effect on other girls. One in particular was sitting in the woodwind section. As soon as she saw Joe, the girl fainted in the middle of her oboe solo. She slid to the floor, oboe still in her mouth, letting out a weak note as she fell.

Accustomed to this reaction, Joe made a beeline for Mr. Phelps. He had a plan to put into motion. "Excuse me," he said. "Hi, I'd like to join the orchestra."

Mr. Phelps stared at the young man in front of him. Like all the faculty, the orchestra teacher was well aware of who Joe was.

"I'm sorry, I don't allow late adds to the orchestra, and you'll get no VIP treatment here, young man," Mr. Phelps told Joe flatly. He was about to tell Joe to leave when a thought occurred to him. Perhaps he could use this "rock 'n' roller" after all. "Unless . . ." he began.

Joe saw his last chance with Angelina flash before his eyes. He jumped. "Unless?!" he cried.

"Well, there is one particular percussion instrument for which I've yet to find a sucker—" Mr. Phelps caught himself. "—candidate . . ." he finished.

Jackpot! Percussion was a breeze. Joe could play the drums, which meant that whatever Mr. Phelps laid on him would would be a piece of cake. His chances with Angelina were looking up. Glancing over at her, he grinned. "Lay it on me!" he told the teacher. "They don't call me Danger for nothing."

Mr. Phelps smiled contentedly. Joe had no clue what he had just signed up for. . . .

Moments later, the orchestra was back to practicing. Joe sat patiently, waiting for his solo. When it came, he enthusiastically struck his new instrument . . . the triangle. Right on cue, a loud *ding!* filled the room. He smiled proudly at Angelina, who barely noticed. The triangle wasn't exactly what he'd had in mind, but Joe was going to rock out as hard as possible. He didn't have any other choice.

As the song continued, Joe started getting into the music. He wanted Angelina to see that he could be a normal orchestra guy. He started inching his way toward where Angelina was playing.

As he went, Joe bumped into various elbows, causing bows to screech across violin strings and the melody to take a turn for the worse. He clanked against music stands and was starting to cause a serious scene when he finally reached his goal: Angelina.

She looked over at him. "What are you doing here?" she whispered angrily.

"I just came over to say hi," he said, flashing his million-dollar smile. "Hi."

Angelina was no fool. "Did you join the orchestra just so you could flirt with me?" she asked.

Joe was in a bit of a panic. How could his plan

have backfired already? "Of course not!" he exclaimed.

Angelina wasn't buying it. Joe was disrupting her favorite thing—orchestra—just so he could flirt with her! She had had enough. No more Miss Nice Girl.

"It's one thing to ask me out in the hallway and not take no for an answer, but I'm serious about my music, and you're interrupting the whole orchestra."

As she spoke the words, the entire orchestra stopped playing. There was dead silence as everyone turned and listened.

"I *don't* want to go out with you!" she added.

She turned around, abruptly picked up her bow, and started to play again. Rejected once again, and this time in front of a roomful of people, Joe weakly hit his triangle, making a sad *ding*.

"Man, I wish that song was three seconds longer," he said, shaking his head sadly.

CHAPTER EIGHT

Orchestra rehearsal continued, despite Joe's crushed dreams. He sat in the percussion section, sadly *ding*ing his triangle to the music. With all hope of landing a date with Angelina fading, Joe needed reinforcements: his brothers. He had texted them as soon as the music had started up again.

After getting Joe's desperate text message, Nick and Kevin rushed to the orchestra room.

They snuck in and made their way over to Joe.

While Nick managed to make it to Joe without causing a huge scene, Kevin wasn't as lucky. As he headed toward his brother, he caused several woodwind players to hit notes that were *definitely* not right. Luckily, Mr. Phelps was busy and didn't notice the intrusion.

"What's the emergency?" Nick asked when he got to his brother's side.

"This is not working. I joined the orchestra, and Angelina hates me even more for it!" Joe couldn't believe how badly things were turning out.

After managing to squeeze past another oboe player—and only knocking half the music off her stand—Kevin arrived. He had an idea.

"I guess, then, we're going to have to talk you up in front of her!" He raised his voice and tilted his head in Angelina's direction. "Tell her how *awesome* of a guy you are!" Kevin leaned in closer to his brothers with a confused look on his face. "I didn't do that right, did I?"

"No," Nick said, shaking his head.

Mr. Phelps looked up from conducting and tapped his baton on the music stand to get the brothers' attention. "Excuse me," he said, his voice full of disdain. "The only *annoying* noise I permit in here is by the orchestra!"

Facing expulsion from the class, Nick acted fast. "Cool," he said cheerfully. "In that case, sign us up!"

Mr. Phelps was flabbergasted. It was hard enough getting kids to sign up for orchestra at the beginning of the year, and today, not one but three were begging to be admitted. What on earth was going on?

"Really? Three professional musicians want to join my orchestra all on the same day? Is this a joke?" he asked, looking around. "Oh! I get it. I get it. I'm being *Punk'd*, right?" He was expecting a camera crew to jump out any minute. When no cameras appeared, he turned to Nick. "All right, I'll play along," Mr. Phelps said. "What do you guys want to play?"

Mr. Phelps wasn't going to trip up Nick. He, like his brothers, was a trained musician, and he knew a thing or two about classical, orchestra-friendly pieces. "Anything by Mozart would be nice."

Kevin jumped in. "Oh, and if we could stay away from *Peter and the Wolf*. Wolves scare me. And I'm not too sure about that Peter, either."

Mr. Phelps shook his head and looked at Kevin and Nick sternly. "I meant which *instrument*," he said.

"Oh, that," Kevin responded.

He picked up a trombone. He put his lips to the mouthpiece, extended the slide, and blew as hard as he could. The force of his breath shot the slide clear out of the instrument and all the way across the room.

Trying a different brass instrument, Kevin grabbed the French horn. He started to play a terrible, screechy tune. That was when Nick and Joe noticed that Kevin's hand was stuck in the flared bell of the horn. They started tugging on it as Kevin continued to play. Finally, the French horn came free and it, too, flew across the room.

The last instrument Kevin tried was the bass drum. He picked up a mallet and with a little too much force slammed it against the drum, breaking the skin with a dull thud and a pop.

Watching his lovable brother fail so miserably at all these instruments made Nick smile. Luckily, he knew exactly which one would make Kevin shine.

"Here, try this," Nick said, handing him a guitar. "Remember, it's the side with the strings on it."

Kevin grinned. *This* he could handle. He picked up the guitar and began strumming it gracefully. The room grew silent as he played a beautiful classical song.

When he was done, everyone, including Mr. Phelps, began applauding. In fact, Mr. Phelps looked quite relieved not to be subjected to Kevin slaughtering yet another instrument that afternoon.

"You're in," Mr. Phelps said when Kevin finished and the applause had died down. Kevin's talent was undeniable. Motioning to the first row, Mr. Phelps barked, "Everybody, make way for Kevin. Come on, everybody, slide down."

As the kids shifted down the bench to make room, the boy on the end fell off. Angelina watched him crash to the ground. She rolled her eyes and moved out of the way so Kevin could pass by. As she suspected, rock stars always got whatever they wanted!

As he walked by her, Kevin whispered, "Well, *cello* there!" He smiled. "See what I did? I put 'hello' and 'cello' to—" Kevin suddenly stopped when he saw that Angelina was not amused. "Joe's a really great guy," he said sheepishly and moved on.

With Kevin and his guitar settled into the orchestra, Mr. Phelps turned his attention to Nick. "How about you? What can you play?"

Nick was multitalented. Name it, and he could play it. "Whaddaya got?" he said, challenging Mr. Phelps.

"Piano?" Mr. Phelps said simply.

Without answering, Nick settled in at the piano and started playing a melody. "This one goes out to Angelina in the string section," he said as he began to play.

"My bro is the kindest guy I know. . . . He likes to take things slow. . . . He's just a regular . . . Joe," Nick sang.

Before Nick could get to the chorus of his impromptu love song, Mr. Phelps interrupted him. "Welcome to orchestra," the teacher said.

"Thank you, I'll be here all period," Nick said with a smile.

Tapping the podium again, Mr. Phelps commanded the orchestra's attention. "All right, settle down, people. Now, as you know, the school recital is coming up, and our version of 'The Blue Danube' sounds like cats in wet cement. Yes, I'm looking at *you*, violins. So if we could please just get through it once with no one hurting themselves."

He tapped his baton and started conducting.

The orchestra played a dreary version of the classical song. Joe caught Nick's and Kevin's eyes. They were all thinking the same thing: this was definitely no rock concert. It would be difficult, but the Lucas brothers were determined to make an impression on Angelina. No matter the musical cost.

CHAPTER NINE

Joe's attempts at winning Angelina were going nowhere. Frustrated, he sat hunched over the island in the middle of the Lucases' kitchen. Not sure what to do or say, Nick got a sponge from the sink and started wiping down the counter.

Finally, Nick threw the sponge he'd been using into the sink. Enough cleaning; he needed to get Joe out of this funk.

"Thirty's your limit, bro. I'm cutting you

off," Nick said, pulling the soda bottle clutched tightly in Joe's hand.

"Don't count, man. That's not cool," Joe protested.

As he and Nick were struggling over the soda, Stella walked in, unaware of the downward spiral Joe was currently in.

"Hey, guys. What's up?" she said to the boys.

Kevin was thrilled to see her. "Did you bring the stuff?" he asked Stella.

Stella stopped short, a puzzled look on her face. "What stuff?" she asked, not sure what Kevin was talking about.

What stuff? What *stuff*? Was Stella for real? Flustered, Kevin almost lost his temper. "Joe's in crisis mode!" he shouted. "I texted you an hour ago. I needed you to bring the rainbow-sprinkle donuts and coffee–flavored ice cream!"

Stella's eyes narrowed. Did Kevin say *text*? Running her hands maniacally through her hair, Stella screamed, "Texting! Texting! That's all anybody ever talks—or texts—about!" She had officially cracked. "Don't you realize that there are other ways of communicating with me? Try writing me a note for a change!"

Nick, Joe, and Kevin all stood in complete shock. Had Stella lost her mind? What was the big deal? Nick quickly scribbled a note and handed it to Stella.

Stella took it. "'Stop yelling at us,'" she read out loud.

She looked at her friends' terrified faces, took a deep breath, and ran her hands through her hair again to calm herself down. She felt bad for freaking out the guys, but not being able to text was making her feel crazy.

Stella tried to focus on the task at hand. "I'm fine," she said, trying to breathe evenly. "Everything's fine. Sorry about the yelling. Ice cream and donuts coming right up!"

The brothers watched as Stella rummaged through her purse. She pulled out . . . nothing. With a strange look in her eyes, Stella started "typing" on an imaginary phone.

Nick was a little worried. "Stella, you do realize you don't have a cell phone in your hand, right?" he asked.

Stella looked at her hands, and *poof!* Her imaginary phone was gone. She was back to reality—a reality without texting. It was unbearable!

"I may not have my cell phone but at least I have my sanity!" she cried. She grabbed her purse and headed for the door. Nick thought he noticed her thumbs texting on an imaginary keyboard as she walked out. Something was not quite right with Stella today. He hoped she would act a little more normal when she got back.

Joe quickly returned to his brooding. "I only joined the orchestra so I could impress Angelina. But we've just made things worse," he said, slumping down on the kitchen island in total frustration.

Nick knew they had to fix this. He paced back and forth, racking his brain for a new way to win over Angelina. What was it that she truly didn't like about Joe? Or, better, what did they have in common? Maybe if they could figure that out, they could make some progress.

"Joe, music is the one thing you and Angelina both love," Nick finally said. "Show her how passionate you are, and she'll come around."

Joe perked up. This was a great idea! He started to feel a bit better. Then he saw the triangle and his smile faded.

He picked up the instrument. It dangled pathetically from his hand. "How can I show her my passion for music with *this*?" he asked.

Nick looked at the wimpy instrument. His brother sort of had a point. But no! They could do this! They just needed the right attitude.

"All right," he said. "Let's not be so quick to judge the triangle. In many ways, you and the triangle are a lot alike."

Kevin looked confused. "Three-sided?" he asked. "Made of metal? Really annoying?"

Nick ignored Kevin. He came around the island and put his arm around Joe. "No. Disrespected . . . put down . . ."

Joe was starting to see the picture Nick was painting. He nodded in agreement. "Misunderstood," he added.

Kevin jumped in. "Yeah! Totally," he said. "*And he's made of metal?*"

Joe and Nick exchanged looks. They'd fill Kevin in soon. But first, Joe "Danger" Lucas was going to rock the triangle.

The orchestra room was full of students making last-minute preparations for the performance. Some were practicing chords and scales; the woodwinds were checking their reeds; the string instruments were tuning up. Although nervous, the members of the orchestra were excited and ready. Mr. Phelps, on the other hand, was a mess. He paced back and forth, beads of sweat starting to form on his brow.

"Tonight's the big recital," he said, cracking his knuckles nervously. "And I'm only in a *semisweat*. With any luck, we'll be able to fill a whole row in the auditorium."

As Mr. Phelps finished his halfhearted pep talk, Nick walked up to him. He had a new plan to put into action.

"Mr. Phelps, we've made a couple of adjustments on 'The Blue Danube.' We were wondering if the orchestra could give it a try," he said.

"A few '*adjustments*'? To 'The Blue Danube'?" Mr. Phelps scoffed. "On the night of the concert?" The teacher couldn't believe what he was hearing. Then he paused to think for a moment. Any "adjustment" couldn't be much worse than what the orchestra was already doing. He shrugged, giving in to Nick's request.

Later that night, all the members of the orchestra were decked out in their best duds, ready to test out the new arrangement.

As they began the performance, parents in the crowd started looking at each other, wondering if this was the same orchestra they'd heard every semester before. What had happened? Had Justin Timberlake replaced Mr. Phelps?

As the song continued, Joe got in position on a riser behind the orchestra, triangle in hand, ready to play the meanest triangle solo in the history of triangle solos.

When the spotlight hit him, the girls in the crowd screamed, while the guys pointed and cheered. They only got louder when Joe really started to play. The triangle had never sounded so incredible. Plus, Joe was doing some of his signature moves. He tossed the triangle in the air, caught it, and started playing once again, without missing a beat.

Angelina had been focused on her cello, but as Joe played the triangle and sang, she couldn't take her eyes off him. She was amazed at his transformation from rock star to orchestra king. As she watched in awe, a huge five-foot-high triangle was lowered from the ceiling. *Wow!* This concert had definitely surpassed their usual orchestra performance.

Once the huge triangle was in place, Joe leaped through it with a double backflip. He made a perfect landing on the other side and started playing the massive instrument.

Joe was on fire. He felt better than he did playing sold-out crowds. It wasn't that the music was better than at a JONAS concert, it was that Angelina was beaming at him. Finally, he had made a good impression. And when Joe smiled at Angelina, she *finally* smiled back.

As Joe continued to play, Angelina stood up, playing the cello passionately. She began to move toward him. Their eyes locked as their duet engaged the audience more and more. When the music hit a crescendo in the grand finale, sparklers shot off and illuminated Joe and Angelina. It was the perfect ending.

CHAPTER TEN

When the last note finally faded, there was no question in anyone's mind—the concert had been a huge hit. And the Lucas brothers were doubly happy. Their plan had worked: Angelina finally saw Joe for the awesome guy that he was.

As people left the auditorium, all they were talking about was the amazing duet at the end. Joe, Nick, and Kevin got caught up in a swarm of fans. After signing some autographs, they found each other in the crowd to talk about what had just happened.

"I rocked the triangle so hard!" Joe exclaimed to his brothers.

Just then, Angelina emerged from the crowd. Seeing Joe, she made a beeline for him.

"Cello girl, four o' clock," Nick said as he and Kevin took a step back to give their brother his space.

"Hi, Joe," Angelina said.

"Hi," Joe said uncertainly.

"Your solo was amazing," Angelina told him with a smile.

Joe beamed with pride. Had he finally won her over?

"Sorry I was kind of a snob," Angelina added apologetically. Maybe she had been too harsh, judging Joe on what she'd heard and not on how he acted.

All was forgiven as far as Joe was concerned. "Do snobs eat chocolate tacos? Because we're going to go grab some."

"They're my favorite!" Angelina responded.

"Mine, too!" Joe cried, taking her hand.

What? Kevin was shocked. "They're not *your* favorite. They're *my* favorite," he interjected.

Joe gave him a swift elbow to the ribs while still grinning at Angelina.

Ouch! Kevin rubbed his ribs, confused. "Remember what *Teenster* magazine said?"

Now Nick had to take action. He jabbed Kevin in the ribs again.

Kevin submitted, doubling over in pain. "Never mind. It hurts too much to care," he mumbled.

The next day, the halls of Horace Mantis were once again filled with students. Rounding a corner, Macy bumped right into Nick, Joe, and Kevin. She gulped. "What's up, Macy?" Nick said cheerfully.

Nick Lucas! Nick Lucas was talking to her! She was standing in the middle of JONAS!

"It's . . . It's . . . The Boys Who Shall Not Be Named . . . J-J-J . . ." Macy stammered.

PART ONE

Joe Lucas is taking a quiz to find out just
how well he knows . . . himself!

Duck! The crowd of JONAS fans outside the
firehouse are more than happy to lend the
boys a pen—or dozens!

When Joe's new crush, Angelina, turns him down, he decides to open some fan mail to help him cheer up.

Kevin and Nick hate to see their brother so sad. They need a plan.

"Sign us up!" the brothers tell the orchestra
teacher. Now Angelina will be able to
see a different side of Joe.

A guitar is Kevin's only hope of making
the band!

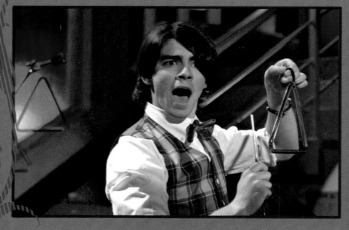

Joe proves that he is always a rock star—
even when playing the triangle.

"Do snobs eat chocolate tacos?" Angelina
asks Joe with a smile. "Because we're
going to go grab some."

PART TWO

The Lucas brothers are ready for game night with their best friend and stylist, Stella Malone.

Kevin is on a roll! He just found a word that will help him win the game!

Nick, Kevin, and Joe listen as Stella tells them exactly how she feels about beauty pageants.

It's showtime! The members of JONAS are enjoying their duties as pageant judges.

Stella shows off her skills when she models the evening gown she made herself.

Nick tries to cheer up Stella after her embarrassing answer to the "Final Question."

The boys have prevented Stella from being
humiliated on national television!

"I just cannot stop thanking you for what
you did for me!" Stella exclaims. Now
she can drop her silly disguise.

Nick tried to encourage her, sounding out their name. "JO-JO-JO . . . ?"

Joe joined in. "What-what-what . . . ?"

As the boys were attempting to help Macy, Stella stormed into the group. She ripped Macy's bag away from her, screaming, "I can't take it anymore!"

She riffled through the bag, digging out her cell phone. Having the phone in her hands felt glorious!

Stella flipped it open and started texting furiously. With every tap she felt happier and happier. "Yes, yes. Good. Texting good. O-M-G." She started cooing to her phone and cuddling it. "I'm here, baby. Mama's here. I'll never leave you again."

In the flurry, Macy realized that Stella had broken the pact. "You're texting. . . . You're texting!" she said, jumping for joy.

Stella didn't care. She was happy, happy, happy to be texting, no matter what the cost. "Yeah, I cracked. Okay? You win. Just leave us alone," she said, holding her phone close to her heart.

Macy was free! Finally! "I can talk!" she cried. She turned to Joe. "JONAS! JONAS! JONAS! Joe of JONAS, can you sign my program from last night's performance?"

"Sure, why not?" Joe said, smiling. "Does anybody have a pen?"

Uh-oh. Big mistake. As soon as the words came out of Joe's mouth, pens came flying at the boys. "Run!" all three cried in unison, and made a beeline for it.

PART
TWO

CHAPTER ONE

Rehearsing music was never a chore for the Lucas brothers. They loved playing together anytime, day or night. Luckily for them, it was easy to rehearse because their bedroom doubled as their own personal recording studio. To some, that might seem a little . . . over the top, but Kevin, Joe, and Nick Lucas weren't just practicing for the high school band, they were practicing for another world tour. Together, the brothers made up the world-famous rock band JONAS.

On this particular day, Kevin was playing an amazing guitar riff while Nick kept the beat on the drums. In typical fashion, Joe, whose nickname was "Danger," added his part by leaping up onto one of the big amps that doubled as a bed frame.

"Check this out!" he shouted before doing his signature flip off the amplifier. As he flew through the air, his sneaker came flying off.

Kevin and Nick watched in horror as the sneaker shot across the room and smashed through the window. They winced as they heard glass shattering, followed by a cat shrieking, the sound of a British ambulance siren, brakes screeching, a cow mooing, and finally, a weak note from a bagpipe somewhere outside.

Had Joe's sneaker caused all that commotion?

The guys were standing in shocked silence when Tom Lucas, their father and manager, popped his head in the bedroom door.

"What's going on up here?" Mr. Lucas cried,

looking a little steamed. "Joe, did you just break the window with a shoe—that then hit a cat, causing a British ambulance to crash and scare a cow, who sat on a fat guy playing bagpipes?"

Uh-oh. Joe was busted. He tried to play it off, gingerly hiding his bare foot behind his other leg.

"No, that was my ringtone," Joe explained, taking out his phone and pretending to answer it. "Hello? . . . It's for you," he said, passing the phone to Nick.

Nick answered it. "Hello?" He listened for a moment before handing the phone to Kevin, shrugging. "It's for you."

Kevin grabbed the phone with a serious look on his face. "Hello?" he said. "Oh, yeah, he's right here. Hold on." He put his hand over the mouthpiece. "Dad, it's for you."

Mr. Lucas looked surprised. "Hello," he said. "Oh, hey, what's going on?"

The boys looked at each other. Wait a minute. . . .

"Is there really somebody on the phone?" Nick asked.

Mr. Lucas grinned slyly and looked straight at his middle son. "I don't know. You tell me, Shoeless Joe."

Joe gulped. There was only one thing he could say. "I'll pay for the window," he promised. And remember to tie my shoes tighter next time, he added silently.

CHAPTER TWO

Later that day, Joe and Kevin sat in their living room playing a board game with their best friend, Stella Malone. She was always there for the guys, whether they needed help with girls, a friend to go to the movies with, or—her personal specialty—fashion advice. She wasn't just their best friend. She was also the band's stylist.

Joe and Stella were waiting impatiently for

Kevin to take his turn. He'd been staring at his letter tiles for what felt like an eternity.

Kevin scratched his head, deep in thought about his next move. Or maybe he was just confused.

Stella couldn't take it anymore. "Kevin, it's been ten minutes. Will you please just *go*?" she begged.

Joe was tired of waiting, too. "Just so you know, no matter how long you stare at those letters, they aren't going to change," he told his older brother.

"Then how did my *Q* just become an *O*?" he asked.

Stella rolled her eyes. Could Kevin really be *that* clueless? "Because I gave that to you," she hissed at him, annoyed.

"JUST GO ALREADY!" Joe shouted.

Kevin dropped the pieces in his hand, startled by the yelling. Just then, Nick, the youngest member of the band, walked in, breaking the tension.

Nick looked over Joe's shoulder at the board. "What are you guys playing?" he asked.

Joe held up the box. "Wordhole," he explained. "It's that Belgian board game we did the commercial for."

JONAS had been hired to promote Wordhole last year. The whole Lucas family had flown to Belgium together and had seen some awesome sights when they weren't filming. Along with the trip, the boys also got to keep a few Wordhole games, which they'd brought home.

"Cool, can I play?" Nick asked, fiddling with some game pieces.

"Too late!" Kevin suddenly shouted. "Because I have a seven-letter word! And I win!"

He started putting his tiles carefully on the board. Everyone watched in anticipation, impressed that Kevin had managed to use all his letters. Stella wondered what Kevin's word could possibly be. Maybe history. Nah, Kevin didn't think too much about history. Could it be *senator*? Nah, he didn't think much about politics, either.

Kevin leaned back from the table, proudly displaying his word. Stella read it aloud. *"Plobnrg?"* She looked up at him. "That's not a word!"

"Sure it is," Kevin said smugly.

"All right, then, what does it mean?" Nick asked.

"It means 'awesome,'" Kevin responded confidently. "Like, 'Hi, I'm Kevin. I just won the board game. I am so *plobnrg.*'"

Joe and Nick both let out a groan. They knew Kevin too well to challenge him on this one.

Just then, Mr. Lucas walked in. He had a big grin on his face and was eager to share some good news with the boys. "Guys, the band just got an exciting offer. It's totally *plobnrg!*"

Joe, Nick, and Stella looked from Mr. Lucas to Kevin in shock. Kevin just shrugged, as if it were no big deal.

Mr. Lucas continued. "How would you boys like to be judges at the Miss Most Amazing Teen competition?"

Joe's mouth dropped open. What could be

better than watching pretty girls strut across a stage? Amazing! "That would be so cool!" Joe cried, unable to contain his enthusiasm.

Kevin liked the idea, too. He was thinking about all the free perks that they would probably get as judges, such as lots of pizza! "Awesome!" he agreed.

Nick was pumped. The contestants for Miss Most Amazing Teen performed in a talent competition, and he was always interested in what impressive things other people could do. Plus, he secretly loved watching baton-twirling.

Suddenly all three boys realized something— Stella was still in the room.

Nick acted the fastest. He cleared his throat and said in a serious tone, "Actually, Dad, we find those contests just glorified beauty pageants." He looked over at his brothers. "Right, gentlemen?"

Kevin caught on. "And superficial and demeaning," he said, trying to sound sincere.

Joe added, "And it sends a bad message to

those hotties"—*Oops!* Joe caught himself—"young women."

Rolling her eyes, Stella finally spoke up. "Guys, spare me. Beauty contests are the only outlet for those poor, pathetic pageant girls whose sole talent is walking in a straight line and waving. Pageants don't bother me," Stella finished, smiling sweetly.

Nick was relieved. "All right, well, I mean, in that case—" he said, trying to contain his excitement.

Kevin cut him off. "I'm in!" he cried.

"Let's do it for the hotties!" Joe said gleefully.

Mr. Lucas glanced at Stella and cleared his throat to let his sons know they should settle down. "Good, it's a go," he confirmed with a nod.

The boys smiled at each other. This was going to be *awesome*.

CHAPTER THREE

The guys didn't waste any time. Kevin, Nick, and Joe were soon walking into the auditorium where the Miss Most Amazing Teen competition was going to be held. They wanted to get the lay of the land—and more importantly, to check out the cute contestants. Wearing sashes, the girls were already strutting their stuff on the stage. Hairdressers were fixing the girls' hair and coaches were reminding them to smile.

Nick looked over at the stage. "So, uh, those must be the girls," he said, trying to sound calm, the way a rock star should.

Joe turned his attention to the front of the hall. "Where?" he asked, pushing his sunglasses down his nose to get a better look. "Oh, there. I didn't notice," he said as nonchalantly as possible.

Seeing that JONAS had arrived, the pageant director made a beeline for them.

The woman definitely looked the part. She was perfectly put together, with a bright pink suit, pink heels, and a matching pink scarf. As she marched toward the boys, she began waving frantically.

"Oh! Hello, gentlemen!" she said when she reached them. "I'm pageant director Maggie Belle Seward. Welcome to the Kream-O Dog Food Superdome, home to this year's Miss Most Amazing Teen competition!" When she finished her introduction, Maggie Belle began applauding as if she'd just introduced the president of the United States.

Kevin looked at his brothers, confused, and started clapping, too. Joe and Nick just stared at Maggie Belle, not sure how to react to her.

Maggie Belle continued. "You probably recognize me . . ." she said and paused, giving the boys a moment to place her.

Introductions over, Maggie Belle walked the boys over to the judges' table. She made a sweeping gesture as if she were Vanna White showing them a big prize. The guys wondered if they were looking at the same thing as Maggie Belle. All they saw was a folding table with a paper tablecloth on it.

"Saturday night, this is where the three of you will be sitting and judging," Maggie Belle said proudly.

Just then, her watch alarm went off. She jumped, a bit startled. "Oh, ticky-tock, it's four o'clock! It's time for me to look in the mirror and give myself a pep talk," she said. She clicked off the alarm and then added, "Otherwise I start crying."

She bowed slightly to the boys and walked off, waving as she went. Kevin started clapping. He glared at Nick and Joe, hinting that they should join in. The three brothers continued to applaud as Maggie Belle made her exit.

"Um, why are we clapping?" Nick asked Joe.

Joe looked confused, too. "I have no idea."

Kevin had the answer. "She's great!" he exclaimed.

Nick and Joe glanced at each other. Kevin sure was a piece of work. They stopped clapping and turned their attention back to what was important—the stage.

"Wow, look at all these girls," Joe said. "They're so good-looking."

Typical Joe, going nuts over girls he barely knows just because they're gorgeous, Nick thought. "Joe, they've got a lot more going for them than looks," he said. "They're poised, they're intelligent. . . ." Nick trailed off, distracted by one of the contestants onstage.

Joe snapped his fingers in front of Nick. It was time to get down to business. Joe was definitely ready to meet and greet the girls. He smiled his "Danger" smile. "Look at her," he said, nodding at a blonde who was doing stretches. "She's really intelligent."

"Which one?" Kevin asked. "I think they're all geniuses," he said admiringly.

"I think we should probably go introduce ourselves," Joe suggested. "I'll start."

Joe started off toward the stage, but Nick grabbed his shoulder. What were these two thinking? This wasn't a social event or a dating service! This was a job, and Nick took his duties very seriously—most of the time.

"We're the *judges*," he pointed out. "We have to be impartial. In fact, we shouldn't have any communication with any of the girls what-soever," he said sternly. Sometimes he wondered if he was the *only* responsible Lucas.

He looked over, ready for his brothers to protest. Wait a second. . . .

"Where's Joe?" he asked Kevin.

Joe was right where he wanted to be: sitting across from Carrie Sue North, a very pretty contestant.

"Well, as a judge, it's my duty to remain impartial. But I'm definitely voting for you," Joe told her as he gazed into her eyes and flashed his trademark smile.

Carrie Sue stood up and stroked Joe's cheek before walking away. After she had taken a few steps, she stopped, turned back, and blew him a kiss. He stood up to "catch it" and in the same swift move pulled back her chair, allowing another contestant to sit down. The new pageant girl batted her eyes and popped her bubble gum.

Joe sat back down. "Well, as a judge, it's my duty to remain impartial," he repeated. "But I'm definitely voting for you."

Smiling happily, the girl stood up and walked away, passing the line of contestants that had formed to have some one-on-one time with Joe Lucas. As yet another girl pulled out the chair to sit down, Nick and Kevin arrived. Without saying a word, the two scooped Joe up by his armpits and carried him off, chair and all.

When they were several feet away, they plopped Joe and the chair down. Nick stood in front of him, his expression stern. "Joe, you can't keep promising every girl that you're going to vote for her!"

Joe pouted for a moment. "Fine," he said, conceding. He was only trying to get to know the very talented contestants . . . and if he happened to flirt with them a little while doing so, what harm was there in that?

Nick knew he had to keep Joe occupied or he would continue to get distracted by all the pretty—and talented—girls. But once again Nick felt that something was wrong. He looked up.

"Where's Kevin?" he asked, frustrated.

Joe knew exactly where their older brother was, and he wished he were in Kevin's place. He pointed behind Nick to where Kevin was sitting with an attractive pageant entrant.

Nick could barely believe his eyes. He stormed over to where Kevin was sitting just in time to hear his brother say, "As a judge, I have to be impartial, but I'm voting for you. *Shh*, don't tell anybody!"

CHAPTER FOUR

The next day, the Lucas brothers were back at school. Kevin was getting books out of his locker and Nick was zipping up his backpack. Suddenly, out of nowhere, a strange yet familiar series of sounds could be heard: a window breaking, followed by a cat shrieking, a British ambulance siren, brakes screeching, a cow mooing, and finally a bagpipe.

Joe pulled out his phone. "That's me," he said,

flipping it open. His eyes grew wide. "Look, one of the contestants just sent me a picture of herself playing flute for senior citizens while saving puppies. What a generous, caring, attractive—"

Nick grabbed Joe's phone from his hand and snapped it in half. Kevin was shocked—Nick must have been working out more lately!

Joe scowled. "You could have just deleted the photo," he complained, trying to stick the two pieces of phone back together.

Just then, Stella walked over. "So, how's the Miss Most Pathetic Teen competition going?" she asked.

Kevin shook his head. "It's the Most *Amazing* Teen competition," he corrected.

Joe rolled his eyes. "She knows that," he told Kevin.

"It's cool," Nick said. "These girls actually have a lot more going on for them than you think."

Stella chuckled. "How sweet," she said insincerely. "And naïve. They don't."

Joe frowned. How could Stella say that about

Carrie . . . and Jennifer . . . and Rachael . . . and Emma? He had to defend their honor! "You just don't understand because you're not the pageant type."

Stella slowly turned to face Joe. "What exactly do you *mean* I'm not the 'pageant type'?" she asked, a dangerous edge to her voice.

"He just means that these girls are beautiful . . ." Nick began.

"And graceful," Kevin added, looking off dreamily into space.

Joe couldn't stay silent. "And really talented," he added. Then he noticed Stella's expression. It looked like smoke might start pouring out of her ears. He gulped. "Not that you're not *all* those things!" he said, but he knew the damage had already been done.

Stella crossed her arms tightly across her chest and gave them her coldest stare. "Those girls are nothing but a bunch of bubbleheaded gorgeous robots," she said. "If I wanted to, I could win that pageant with half my brains tied behind my back!"

Kevin tried to imagine what *that* would look like. "Not a pretty picture," he said, making a face.

Joe looked at Stella and smiled. "Wait a minute. Half your brains hanging out, batting a bunch of beautiful robots?" he said. "Now *that* is a competition I would pay to see!"

Still fuming, Stella took a deep breath. She tried to reassure herself that she was above all this superficial junk.

"I don't need a pageant to tell me I'm just as pretty and talented as any of those girls," she informed the boys. "Not to mention feminine, demure, and very, very delicate. Now, if you'll excuse me . . ." She tried to walk past the guys. But they wouldn't move.

"Make a hole!" she screamed at them. Shocked at her outburst, the brothers scrambled. They'd never seen Stella so worked up. She stormed down the hallway, practically knocking over three freshmen on the way.

CHAPTER FIVE

Later that day, the boys relaxed in their room before getting started on their homework. Joe and Nick were watching TV, and Kevin sat to the side, staring into space. Occasionally he would smile, nod his head, and then stroke his chin as if deep in thought. Even for Kevin, this was strange behavior.

After watching for a few minutes, Joe had to ask. "What are you doing?"

Without breaking his concentration, Kevin responded, "I'm practicing judging." Continuing to "practice," he chuckled as if something were funny. Then he gave a thumbs-up—to nobody.

Maybe Kevin is on to something, Joe thought as he plopped down next to his brother. Joe began to smile at nothing and clap as if something had happened. Wow! He was getting better at this judging thing already. Seeing how much fun his brothers were having, Nick joined them.

As the three brothers continued to mimic all the actions they would have to carry out as judges, they heard a voice coming from the hallway. It was Stella. "Gentlemen," she announced, "the next Miss Most Amazing Teen . . . Stella Malone!"

Kevin, Joe, and Nick turned to see Stella strut into the room, waving and doing her best "pageant" walk. She was even wearing a sash! The boys were shocked.

"What are you doing?" Joe asked Stella.

"I have officially entered the contest," Stella said smoothly as she gave the boys a dazzling smile.

Joe jumped up. "What?!" he asked in shock. Had he heard that right? Stella, a beauty pageant contestant? No way.

"How did you even get in?" Nick asked. "The deadline for entries was weeks ago."

Stella smiled. "For some reason, Maggie Belle decided to allow one extra girl in the competition this year," she said mysteriously. "I'm going to beat these bubbleheaded beautybots at their own game," Stella went on, a competitive glint in her eye. "Not that I care," she added as she started to walk out. If she was going to win, she had some more practicing to do.

"Way to go! That's the attitude!" Joe said, hoping he sounded encouraging.

"You've got to be in it to win it!" Kevin cheered.

"You should really go for it!" Nick added.

"You guys are the best," Stella sang out as she exited the room.

Suddenly, the TV caught the boys' attention. "This Saturday, it's the Miss Most Amazing Teen competition," an announcer was saying, "with special guest judges, JONAS!"

The guys gathered around the TV. Even though they were pretty used to seeing themselves on-screen and hearing their music on the radio or their name announced in concert, they were still thrilled every time.

The commercial continued. "Don't miss five-time pageant champion Carrie Sue North as she takes on all newcomers!"

Joe raised his eyebrows. He hadn't known that he had been flirting with the reigning champion. Maybe he and his brothers should have done some research about the pageant.

Carrie Sue looked beautiful on TV with cameras flashing all around her. "For me," she was saying, "it's not about the competition. It's about enjoying the company of the other girls who are *almost* as 'most amazing' as me. See you Saturday night!"

Then Carrie Sue did an amazing double back

handspring, followed by an entire gymnastics routine, while wearing her gown and sash, without messing up a single perfectly sculpted piece of hair. Wow, no wonder she'd won five times in a row.

The boys looked at each other nervously. "I don't think Stella knows what she's gotten herself into," Joe said.

"This is not going to end well," Nick said to his brothers, shaking his head.

"Whoever told her to go for this is a real doorknob," Kevin put in. His brothers stared at him. "Yes," Kevin continued, "I know it was me."

CHAPTER SIX

The day of the big competition arrived more quickly than the boys, and probably Stella, would have liked. The arena was decorated in full Miss Most Amazing Teen competition regalia. There was a frantic energy in the auditorium and an excitement that was palpable. Pageant staff were running around, making last-minute arrangements; camera crews were setting up; contestants were practicing their walks and readjusting their garments.

Amid all the hustle and bustle, the members of JONAS stood near the judges' table. They were all nervous. Not because of the task at hand—they had done plenty of practicing at home—but because they were all worried that Stella had bitten off more than she could chew.

Scanning the contestants, Joe saw Stella. He caught her eye, and she waved. She looked as happy as a clam.

He forced a smile and waved back. "Look at her," he said to his brothers. "She has no idea she's in way over her head. What are we going to do?"

Kevin smiled and waved at Stella, too. "It's easy. We're the judges. We just vote for her," he said.

Nick smiled widely and gave Stella a big wave. "We can't vote for Stella if she's not the best, no matter how humiliating for her," he said out of the corner of his mouth.

The boys continued to wave happily at Stella. "We've got to talk her out of it," Nick said. The others nodded. It was the only choice. They started walking toward their friend, ready to break the news to her.

Stella smiled as they approached. "Hey, guys, do you like my shoes? I dyed them to complement my eyes," she said, and then somehow managed to stretch her leg so her foot was next to her face.

"Nice match," Joe said kindly. Then his expression grew serious. "Stella, we want to talk to you about the competition."

Nick nodded. "Are you sure you know what you're doing?" he asked.

"These girls have been doing this since they were, like, five years old," Kevin explained. "They're like beauty-queen sharks. They swim up to a competitor, rip her guts out, and then chew and gnaw until there's nothing—"

Nick cut him off. "We get it!" he cried.

Stella put her hand on her hip. "Look, if you guys are worried about me becoming shark food, don't be. I know the secret to winning these things." She stopped and lowered her voice, pulling the guys in closer before continuing. "It's the *final question*," she said with a satisfied smile. "While those bubbleheads are all"—Stella put on her best high-pitched, ditzy voice—"'I personally believe that only through recycling will we ever attain world peace'"—she returned to her normal voice—"I'm going to give an answer with some real meat on its bones. Now if you'll excuse me, I have to work on my evening gown. . . ."

Stella picked up a huge swatch of blue fabric and a small sewing kit. If anyone could whip up a dress in an afternoon, it was Stella Malone.

Just then, Carrie Sue North walked by. She'd overheard the last part of their conversation, and she had a great big smile plastered on her face. She looked Stella straight in the eye. "If I were you, I'd work on getting rid of that zit on your nose," she said smugly. Then she stopped for a second and coughed.

Nick cocked his head. Had Carrie Sue just said "loser" under her breath?

Stella smiled sweetly. "I happen to know that

I'm zitless. But *you* should really get that piece of spinach between your teeth," she said before bundling up her fabric and walking off to finish her gown.

"Nice try," Carrie Sue said as Stella disappeared. But as soon as Stella was out of sight, Carrie Sue flipped open her phone and started frantically pushing buttons. "Dental team. Code three!" she yelled into the mouthpiece.

CHAPTER SEVEN

That evening the stage was set for the big competition. As the lights dimmed, the audience quieted down, relaxing into their seats. Spotlights started to swirl around the dark stage. Two huge projectors in the wings were turned on, beaming the pageant logo out over the audience. The effect was awesome.

A voice boomed over the loudspeakers, greeting everyone: "Live from the Kream-O Dog

Food Arena, it's the eighteenth annual Miss Most Amazing Teen competition. Here's your host, Mark DeCarlo!"

The evening's host walked out onstage, waving at the audience and smiling. "Hello, everyone, I'm Mark DeCarlo!" He waited for a ripple of applause from the audience. None came.

He forged on. "Tonight, we are truly honored to have an incredible panel of celebrity judges from the hottest band in the world, JONAS. Please welcome Joe, Nick, and Kevin!" he shouted and pointed toward the judges' table, which was suddenly illuminated by two spotlights.

The audience erupted in applause. Girls jumped up and down, screaming. Two fans rushed the stage and had to be grabbed by security. One girl got so excited she fainted in the aisle. The brothers smiled and waved calmly at the crowd from their seats.

Attempting to be heard over the screaming fans, Mark DeCarlo continued, "All right. We've got our judges, you got me, what are we missing? The lovely ladies. Let's meet them, shall we?"

As the pageant band played, the contestants began to walk out onto the stage, waving. Each one looked over at the judges, and each one— except Stella—gave JONAS a big wink. Joe and Kevin gave them each a big wink back. Nick jabbed both of his brothers in the ribs with his elbows. They were hopeless!

During the first portion of the competition, the girls modeled evening gowns. This was definitely Kevin's favorite part; he'd always appreciated a well-crafted ball gown. The competitors all looked stunning as they crossed the stage.

Stella stood in the wings getting ready to make her entrance. Her dress had come out beautifully. Even *she* was impressed with herself. Unfortunately, Carrie Sue had also recognized that Stella's dress was one of a kind. In the wings, the five-time champion gave a swift nod and an evil grin to her accomplices—two other pageant contestants—who were standing behind Stella.

Stella's name was called, and as soon as she started to walk out, the two girls stepped on the train of her gown. There was a loud *RIP!* Stella looked down to see the train completely ruined. She glared at the two girls. But there wasn't time for revenge. She quickly pulled the train up and twisted it around her waist until the gown looked even better than it had before!

Stella lifted her head high and proudly walked across the stage. The crowd took notice, *oohing* and *ahhing* over her gown. Nick, Joe, and Kevin were impressed. They knew she had style—after all, she *was* their stylist—but Stella had really stepped it up. Maybe she had a chance in this competition, after all!

Unlike his brothers, Nick was most excited about the talent portion. He knew these girls were more than just beauties, and he wanted to see what they could do.

The first contestant up was a baton twirler.

She was quite impressive—until she let out a huge sneeze. The baton went flying straight toward the brothers! They ducked under the judges' table just in time. Behind them, the baton plunged into the wall, where it stuck straight out, right where Kevin's head would have been. The three boys gulped. That had been a little too close for comfort.

The next contestant came out onstage with a strange variety of items. She had stacks of folded clothes, a toothbrush, a hair dryer, a few pairs of shoes, and a very small carry-on suitcase. Joe and Nick looked at each other, puzzled. There was no way she was going to fit everything into *that* bag.

But just like that, the girl started packing furiously. She stuffed, pulled, jammed, ripped, snapped, zipped, and buckled, and somehow managed to fit everything in the bag! Finally, she bent over and delicately pulled the last zipper closed. Kevin couldn't believe his eyes. Now that was some serious talent!

The audience applauded. Nick, Joe, and Kevin

were impressed. Where was this girl when their mom told them to hurry up and get packed for a tour?

The talent portion was almost over, and the audience was getting a bit restless. There were only so many baton-twirling acts that one could see before getting . . . well, bored. Stella was one of the last to go, and she was waiting in the wings for her turn.

"Our next contestant in the talent competition is Miss Stella Malone," Mark DeCarlo finally announced.

The three brothers crossed their fingers under the table, hoping that their friend would dazzle the crowd. "I hope she came up with a good talent!" Joe whispered.

"She's been doing great so far," Nick said, though he was keeping his fingers—and his toes—crossed.

"Please don't stink. Please don't stink. Please don't stink," Kevin chanted under his breath.

Stella walked out to center stage barefoot.

With all the showmanship she could muster, she pulled out two cell phones and showed them to the audience before placing them on the floor. Then she pulled out two more cell phones. Audience members began looking at each other, not sure what to make of this act.

Mark DeCarlo also had a quizzical look on his face. The host flipped through his note cards somewhat frantically, searching for the one with Stella's talent. When he finally found it, he read aloud: "Stella's talent is . . . multi-texting."

"I believe communication is the key to our future," Stella explained as she sat down, positioning her feet so her toes could reach each cell phone on the floor. Stella began texting on all four phones simultaneously—one with each hand and one with each foot. It was quite an impressive sight. With an air of finality, she then pressed SEND on all four phones at once.

Two seconds later, Nick's, Joe's, Kevin's, and Mark's cell phones beeped. The crowd was silent as each guy pulled out his phone. They all had one new text message from Stella! Joe had trouble reading the message because his phone was held together with two strips of duct tape, thanks to the fact that Nick had snapped it in half earlier. Nevertheless, he was seriously impressed.

The audience went crazy. Stella even got a few people up on their feet cheering. Kevin, Joe, and Nick looked at each other in relief. If Stella could keep this up, she just might have a shot at the crown!

CHAPTER EIGHT

The pageant was quickly drawing to a close. Stella had made it all the way to the dreaded "final question." If she answered well, she had a real shot at showing Carrie Sue that *she* was Miss Most Amazing Teen.

Once again, Mark DeCarlo took center stage. "Coming up next, our final question. But first, a word from our sponsor, Wordhole . . . the *plobnrg* Belgian word game that's sweeping the nation!"

Nick and Joe looked at each other. Wordhole? *Plobnrg?* What were the odds?

Backstage, the contestants attended to last-minute preparations. Most of the girls had small entourages surrounding them, including people who were fixing their makeup, touching up their hair, and adjusting their outfits.

Stella, on the other hand, was on her own, doing her makeup herself. But as she looked at her makeup case, she noticed that something seemed off. Looking closer, she realized that something was *definitely* wrong with her foundation. It just didn't look like her usual color. Stella lifted it closer to her face and took a sniff. And why did it smell like graham crackers?

Stella looked around at the other contestants. "Who put graham crackers in my foundation?" she demanded

The other girls didn't even bother to *pretend* to care. They just snickered as their teams continued to touch them up.

Stella had had enough. "All right, ladies.

You've been messing with me all night. But that just means you're scared of me," she observed. "Now it's time for the final question, and the winner is going to be someone with a brain. Maybe if you all put your heads together, you can come up with one." Then she added sweetly, "See you in the spotlight," before sauntering off.

Back at the judges' table, Nick, Joe, and Kevin were conferring before the pageant's last segment began.

"Can you believe how good Stella's been doing?" Nick asked his brothers.

"All she has left now is the final question," Kevin said, nodding.

"And we know she's going to ace that," Joe said. Stella had certainly made it clear that the final question would be her time to shine. Plus, they had heard her talk—a lot—over the years, and she could be very convincing.

Finally, the waiting was over. Mark DeCarlo came back out on the stage, the girls falling in line behind him.

"Congratulations to all our competitors for making it this far. It's now time for the final question," he said ominously. "So much of their score depends on how the ladies answer their final question that it renders everything that has happened in the show up to this point completely meaningless. Backstage, we played Rock-Paper-Scissors to determine who would flip a coin to discover which two contestants would thumb wrestle to be the first to answer the final question. Then we realized that was ridiculous and decided just to pick a name out of this glass bowl."

The band played a few foreboding notes as Mark fished around in the bowl. He picked out a piece of paper and read from it. "Stella Malone," Mark announced, "come on down!"

Stella smiled brightly and joined the host at center stage. He handed her a microphone and flipped over a card to read her the question.

"All right, Stella Malone, this is your final question. In your opinion, what is the most pressing problem facing our country today?"

At the judges table, the brothers' faces lit up. This was a no-brainer for Stella. She would totally nail this answer!

"Stella, we're on television," Mark reminded her. Suddenly, the band started playing, and eerie, dramatic music filled the room. The spotlight shone down directly on Stella's face. She looked out into the audience, at all those people leaning forward, anxiously awaiting her response. Stella felt her palms start to get sweaty. Her heart began beating furiously.

Mark looked up from the card—wasn't she going to say something? "Stella?" he asked, trying to snap her out of it.

But Stella was paralyzed, her wide eyes fixed on the audience.

Finally, Stella caught her breath and began. "I personally believe that . . . uh . . ." she stammered. "Today's most pressing problem," she said, taking a deep breath, "um, is U.S. Americans are unable to do so, because some people out there in our nation don't *have* maps, and I believe our education, such as in Africa and Australia, everywhere like, such as, and should help Australia and Europe's . . ." She was stumbling so much she didn't know what to say next. Finally, she shrugged. "World peace," she said, hanging her head in defeat.

Over at the judges' table, the guys couldn't believe what had just happened. That was a disaster! Kevin had his hands over his eyes. He hadn't been able to watch it. Joe had his hands over his mouth. He had to stop himself from screaming. And Nick had his hands over his ears. It was just too painful to hear her struggle. One thing was for sure—Stella had blown the final question . . . and the competition!

CHAPTER NINE

The pageant was over. Inside the auditorium, people were lowering banners, moving monitors, and folding up tables. The night had been quite overwhelming—for more than one contestant.

Stella was slumped in a heap backstage, completely devastated. She was so upset that she'd stopped noticing the snickering of people passing by her. Everyone had seen her complete disaster of an answer. World peace! She kept replaying it in her mind. That was the lamest answer ever! Not to mention the nonsense that had come before!

Nick, Joe, and Kevin had finished up their judging duties and were now trying to comfort their friend. But it wasn't working. Stella was in a trance.

Just then, Carrie Sue walked by, wearing a huge crown and carrying a bouquet, and followed by some of her doting fans. She noticed Stella on the floor. Stopping next to her, Carrie Sue turned to her followers. "And look, if it's not the little geography major," she said, tilting her head toward Stella. "Like I've always said, people who aren't pageant types shouldn't compete in pageants," she announced loudly.

Her followers started laughing mindlessly. Carrie smiled smugly and led them away to celebrate her victory. It was too much. Stella broke down sobbing.

Joe put his arm around her. "We voted for you . . . in our hearts," he told Stella.

"But technically, we had to use the ballots," Nick added.

Kevin tried to do his part to ease the pain. "So, it's only *officially* that you're a loser," he said cheerfully.

Nick shot him a look that clearly said "You're *not* helping."

Stella looked up, still sobbing uncontrollably. "Thank you," she said between sobs. "I don't know what happened. I mean, I just blanked. I looked out at the audience and all I saw were . . ." She trailed off.

"Headlights?" Joe asked. He knew how she felt. Although he was over his stage fright, Joe could still remember that feeling.

Stella nodded. "Yeah, and I felt like . . ."

"A deer in them?" Nick asked, finishing her thought. He knew that feeling, too.

She nodded again, trying to hold back the tears. "You guys were right. I should have known I don't belong here with these girls."

Nick shrugged. "Like you said, the only reason

113

these girls are so good at these competitions is because it's all they've got going for them."

"Yeah, that and all the boyfriends and fancy cars and big houses and magazine covers," Kevin added. Then, noticing his brothers glaring fiercely at him, he stopped. "Sorry," he said. But he couldn't help adding, "And movie deals."

Joe jumped in. "Stella," he said sincerely, "I think you're beautiful and really funny and way cooler than any girl here."

Stella sniffed. "Really? You think I'm beautiful, Joe?" she asked, her cheeks turning slightly red.

Joe's turned even redder. "I meant we *all* do," he corrected.

"It doesn't matter. This thing's going to be all over the Internet!" she wailed into a crumpled tissue. "By tomorrow morning, the whole world is going to be laughing at me!" It was just too much to handle. She got up and ran off.

Joe sighed. "We should have tried harder to talk her out of this."

Nick felt awful. "We can't let this happen to

114

our best friend. We have to fix this." There *had* to be something JONAS could do to help.

Kevin nodded in agreement. Then he shrugged. "At least she cries like a winner," he said.

CHAPTER TEN

Stella still hadn't recovered from her total humiliation when she arrived at school the next day. And worse, it seemed like people were watching the video on every computer in school!

Foreseeing the embarrassment, Stella had prepared. She was dressed in a "disguise"—a scarf and dark sunglasses. Spotting Joe, Nick, and Kevin, she quickly walked over.

"Everybody is watching the video!" she cried.

"I'm going to have to move to a town where there's no Internet. I'm going to be going to school on a donkey!"

The brothers shared a knowing look. "All right, before you go donkey shopping, why don't you check out what everyone's *really* watching?" Nick said.

"It's not what you think. Watch," Joe added.

Stella frowned in confusion as Nick pulled out his laptop. He opened it and revealed the screen.

A music video by JONAS began playing. And that video featured none other than . . . Stella herself! Stella gasped. The guys had spliced together parts of her answer to the final question with a new song they'd written. They'd actually managed to take pieces of her confusing answer and make them sound sensible! The song rocked, and Stella sounded smart—and like she could rap!

Stella was in complete shock. "You guys actually found a way to make my flub look cool!" she exclaimed. She couldn't believe her friends had gone to all this trouble to save her reputation.

"There's already over eight million hits on the video, plus people don't even care what happened at the pageant," Kevin told her, smiling.

"I don't know how to thank you guys," Stella said, amazed.

Joe shrugged. "It was nothing."

Nick smiled. "Yeah, we just stayed up all night writing a song, recording it, assembling a camera crew, and editing all the footage together," he said. "But it was really nothing."

Stella was beaming. She grabbed her friends as tightly as she could for a group hug. "You guys are the best! Thank you. You know how much I hate looking silly."

Feeling flattered and confident, she began to walk away. Unfortunately, she was a little too distracted to notice the giant Dumpster in the middle of the hall. She flopped head over heels into the bin and landed with her feet sticking straight up into the air. Then the bin, with Stella's flailing body still inside, started rolling down the hallway. Every student there saw it. Some people had even whipped out their cell phones and recorded Stella's tumble into the garbage.

The guys looked at each other, knowing full well that they had another Stella disaster on their hands. Nick scratched his head. "I'll go write a song," he said.

Joe pulled out his cell phone. "I'll call the camera crew."

Sighing, the brothers peeled off in different directions to start the damage control and save Stella's reputation for the second time that week. After all, the members of JONAS were loyal to their best friend—even when she was covered in trash.

Don't miss a chance to see
more of the Jonas Brothers
in Hannah Montana.

Hit or Miss

Adapted by Laurie McElroy

Based on the series created by Michael Poryes and Rich Correll & Barry O'Brien

Based on the episode, "Me And Mr. Jones And Mr. Jones And Mr. Jones," Written by Douglas Lieblei

Miley Stewart drummed her fingers against the wall and let out a big sigh. She was dressed as Hannah Montana in the hallway of a recording studio. The red neon sign above the studio door was lit. A sign on the door read: Do Not Enter When the Red Light Is On. Whoever was in the studio was eating into her recording time, and she was getting impatient. She stood up and paced the hall, frowning.

Miley's father, Robby Ray Stewart, wasn't nearly as worked up. He was doing a crossword puzzle to pass the time. "Five-letter word: sixth president of the United States," he said.

Instead of answering, Miley groaned.

"That would work if his name was John Quincy *Ugh*," her father joked.

Miley shook her head. "Dad, I need to record now! What is taking so long?" she demanded. "Hannah is in the zone."

Hannah Montana was Miley Stewart's alter ego. By day, Miley was just like any other high-school girl. By night, she was pop-music sensation Hannah Montana. Miley loved being Hannah onstage. Offstage, she wanted to be able to hang with her friends, go to school, and to the mall. Miley wanted people to like her for who she was, and not just because she was famous.

In order to do that, she kept her Hannah Montana identity a secret. When she was Hannah, Miley covered her long, brown, wavy hair with a blond wig, and traded in her t-shirt and jeans for glamorous sequins and leather jackets.

Mr. Stewart was Hannah's songwriter and manager. He wore a disguise, too—a mustache and a hat. He knew his daughter well enough to recognize the real reason for her impatience. It had nothing to do with being in the zone, and *everything* to do with shopping.

"So what time is that big shoe sale you're meeting Lilly at?" he asked.

"Three-thirty," Miley admitted. "And you know all the sixes go first!"

"No, honey, I'm proud to say I don't know that," Mr. Stewart told her. "Now what you need to do is just relax. Whoever is in there is just running a little late. They'll be done any minute."

Miley didn't want to relax. She wanted to record her song and get to that shoe sale. "They'll be done sooner than a minute," she said, grabbing the door handle.

"Hey!" Mr. Stewart yelled, trying to stop her.

But he was too late. Miley had opened the door and marched into the recording studio.

A sound technician sat behind a panel of recording equipment. Three guys sat in a soundproof booth behind a glass window, putting the finishing touches on a song.

"Okay, who do you think you are?" Miley yelled, "The—"

She stopped short when she saw who was recording. She recognized their faces. "Sweet mama!" she exclaimed. "It's the Jonas Brothers!"

The Stewarts had moved from Tennessee to a beach house in Malibu, California, a few years ago, but that didn't stop Miley from lapsing into a Tennessee twang when she was surprised. Miley might have been a teen superstar, but she was also a teenage girl — *and* a big fan.

Kevin, Joe, and Nick Jonas were staring through the glass at her, wondering why she had interrupted their recording session.

Miley quickly pulled herself together and tried to act as if she wasn't the one who had barged into a recording session. "Daddy, I told you somebody was in here," she said over her shoulder. Then she flipped a switch on the soundboard so the guys could hear her. "I am so sorry, guys. He gets so impatient."

Mr. Stewart walked in, rolling his eyes. "Sorry, fellas, I've got a big shoe sale I need to get to," he said wryly.

Nick Jonas hit his brother Joe on the arm. "Dudes, it's Hannah Montana!" he exclaimed.